For overcoming their fear of dogs, and inspiring me,
this book is dedicated to Aggie, Kendal, Emma, and Sarah E. —S. P.

To Andrew and Peter, my fearless sons. —L. D.

Text copyright © 2006 by Susanna Pitzer
Illustrations copyright © 2006 by Larry Day

First published in the United States of America in 2006 by
Walker Publishing Company, Inc.
Distributed to the trade by Holtzbrinck Publishers

For information about permission to reproduce selections from this book, write to Permissions, Walker & Company, 104 Fifth Avenue, New York, New York 10011.

Library of Congress Cataloging-in-Publication Data

Pitzer, Susanna.
Not afraid of dogs / Susanna Pitzer ; illustrations by Larry Day.
p. cm.
Summary: Young Daniel must confront his fear of dogs when his mom dog sits his aunt's pet.

ISBN-10: 0-8027-8067-9 (hardcover)
ISBN-13: 978-0-8027-8067-6 (hardcover)
ISBN-10: 0-8027-8068-7 (reinforced)
ISBN-13: 978-0-8027-8068-3 (reinforced)
[1. Fear—Fiction. 2. Dogs—Fiction.] I. Day, Larry, 1956- ill. II. Title.
PZ7.P6893Not 2006 [E]—dc22 2005027500

The illustrations for this book were created using pen and ink with watercolor and gouache on watercolor paper.

Book design by Nicole Gastonguay

Visit Walker & Company's Web site at www.walkeryoungreaders.com

Printed in China

10 9 8 7 6 5 4 3 2

Not Afraid of DOGS

Susanna Pitzer

Illustrations by
Larry Day

Walker & Company
New York

"I'm the bravest boy of all!" said Daniel. "I'm not afraid of spiders. I'm not afraid of snakes. I'm not even afraid of thunderstorms."

"You're afraid of dogs," said his sister, Jenny.

"I'm not afraid of dogs," said Daniel. "I just don't like them."

"Don't be a 'fraidy cat," said Jenny.

"I'm not a 'fraidy cat!" said Daniel. "I'm the bravest boy of all."

Daniel shut his door and locked it.

But Daniel didn't know what to do when he came home and found his mom holding one.

"Mom! I don't like dogs!"

"I know, honey, but Aunt Rose had to go on a trip. Bandit has no other place to stay."

Daniel stayed away from dogs. He crossed the street when he saw one. He left the playground if a dog was there. He took the stairs if one was on the elevator.

Dad came home and Daniel ran to greet him. But when Daniel saw Bandit, he raced back to his room.

"Daniel, what's wrong?" called Dad.

"He's afraid of dogs," said Jenny.

"I'm not afraid of dogs!" yelled Daniel. "I just don't like them."

Daniel sat alone in his room.

"Time for supper!" called Mom.
"I'm not hungry!" called Daniel.
"He's afraid," said Jenny.
"Am not!" yelled Daniel.

Mom brought Daniel a plate of food. "Honey, you have to come out sometime. Bandit won't hurt you."

Daniel just closed his door.

That night, Daniel had to go to the bathroom. Outside, he heard a loud thunderstorm.

"I'm the bravest boy of all," thought Daniel. "Even thunderstorms don't scare me."

Daniel opened his door a crack—no Bandit in sight. He ran into the bathroom. "Whew! Safe."

"Oooooooouuuuuuwwwww,"

cried Bandit from behind
the toilet.

Daniel was too scared to move.

There was a clap of thunder. Bandit
yelped and ran under Daniel's legs.
Daniel screamed and jumped into the
bathtub.

Bandit tried to jump in too, but she wasn't
big enough.

"Stay away," said Daniel. His heart pounded.
"Oooooouuuuuuwwwww," cried Bandit.

Daniel and Bandit stared at each other.
Then Daniel's eyebrows crinkled. "You're not
after me. You're afraid of thunderstorms."

"Ooooooouuuuuwwww," cried Bandit.

Daniel's voice softened. "Don't be scared." He slowly reached his hand over the tub.

With one finger, Daniel touched Bandit's shaking back. Her fur was soft.

Bandit licked his finger. Daniel jerked it back. It tickled.

Daniel climbed out of the bathtub
and knelt down. "It's all right, Bandit."
"Oouuww."

Daniel picked her up.

His heart was beating fast. He'd
never held a dog before.

Bandit stopped yowling.

Daniel carried Bandit into his room and put
her on the bed. "You can sleep with me tonight."
Bandit stopped shaking. She snuggled
beside Daniel and fell asleep.

"I'm the bravest boy of all," thought Daniel.
"I'm not afraid of spiders. I'm not afraid of
snakes. I'm not even afraid of thunderstorms.
And—I do like dogs."